Wilmslow Road

By Robert Z. Williams

Disclaimer: The people in this story are fabricated.

Introduction:

Wilmslow Road runs south from the city of Manchester. The busiest bus corridor in Europe it passes the city's university and runs through areas of mixed affluence from *Hathersage Road* to *Parrs Wood*. Unemployment is high in *Fallowfield*, a suburban settlement of 15,000 inhabitants lying 3 miles from the city centre. It has a couple of bars, a large grocery store, some fast food joints and an illegal massage parlour that is allowed to operate by the local police. This is the story of Mac and the boys who frequent *Lloyd's Bar* preferring its cheap prices and bohemian atmosphere to *The Houses of Parliament*; the latter a more respectable bar situated on the other side of *Wilmslow Road* which doesn't open until midday. This is a story about students, bums, gamblers and whores, or saints, holy men, martyrs and angels depending on your point of view.

For the amoral fringe personified by Mac and the boys, life expectancy is low, suicide rates are high, and legal employment is often seen as a last resort in the absence of decent jobs. Yet beautiful young female students abound and being served a drink by one of these sirens is Mac and the boy's daily consolation though realistically they have more chance of sex in Dora's massage parlour. There are no dreamers in *Lloyd's Bar*. Mac and the boys accept reality for what it is and not what they would like it to be. This is a story about Mac and the boys and the day to day struggle for survival on *Wilmslow Road*.

Chapter 1

Each day at 8am the manager of *Lloyd's Bar* opens its doors to serve breakfast. Alcoholic drinks are served at 9am and some hard core locals drift in early doors for liquid refreshment. Nobody knows who gave *Lloyd's Bar* its name but it has always been referred to that way despite its official name being *The Cosmopolitan*.

Two-Guns sipped on his first pint of cider and looked out of the window. He chuckled to himself watching as cars steered to avoid huge pot holes and student cyclists swerved recklessly in and out of traffic. Two-Guns had been awake since day break waiting for *Lloyd's* to open, just as the urban fox was finishing its night time scavenging and returning to its lair in *Platt Fields Park*. There wasn't anything predatory about Two-Guns, an ex-railway worker with a decent pension. It was just that he found sleeping difficult and was always the first of the gang to arrive in the pub. Mac and the rest of the boys would start to drift in later.

As he bided his time waiting for his friends Two-Guns watched the cleaning woman enter Dora's massage parlour which abuts *Lloyd's Bar*. He knew that Dora and the girls would be safely tucked up in their own beds by now. He also knew from experience that it was too early for the bums to start emerging from the nearby flop house, *The Handsdown Hotel*. Two-Guns was happy that he had a nice apartment having served his apprenticeship in places like *The Handsdown* when he was a young man. You make your own luck in this world, he thought to himself with self satisfaction. As if to underline the maxim Two-Guns noticed the resident pan handler across the road. He had taken up his seated pitch by the entrance to *Blueberry's* grocers and alongside the Rumanian vendor was already busily selling her homeless magazines.

The rush hour traffic had started to slacken and it was time for the village idiot to start his daily performance which Two-Guns secretly enjoyed. Kevin Spacey as he was ironically known, largely because he bore resemblance to the disgraced actor, had started to climb the traffic lights. Mac saw Spacey as he emerged from the bookie's but was immune to his antics. Spacey who wore a plant pot on his head adorned with reflective mirrors, to counteract alien death rays, was now shouting abuse at passing cars. Spacey was not allowed in *Lloyd's Bar* and had been barred for life. Head down Mac made a beeline for *Lloyd's* as the mad man mounted a *Belisha beacon* and started to simulate a sexual act.

"I see Spacey is on form this morning," said Mac as he sat down next to Two-Guns with his opening pint of lager.

"Yeah, he wants locking up," replied Two-Guns.

The two men lapsed into silent contemplation while wiping the condensation from their pint glasses.

"Have you had a bet, Mac?" asked Two-Guns.

"Only a small one," replied Mac.

"How much?"

"A fiver each way on a horse at Chepstow."

"What odds?"

"Eights."

Two-Guns was known for his mindless questioning not that ridicule deterred him.

"When do you sign on again?" asked Two-Guns.

"I'm on the sick now and got a sick note for three months but you know this. I told you yesterday," replied Mac.

"So what are you having for tea tonight then?"

"For fucks sake Two-Guns, can a man not drink his pint in peace?"

"I won't say another word," said Two-Guns looking slightly offended.

Two-Guns stayed silent until Wes and The Artist, the last of the *Four Musketeers*, simultaneously arrived. Wes was first to speak, his address aimed at Two-Guns.

"I had tea and toast for breakfast. Last night I polished off egg and chips and tonight I am planning on baked potatoes with cheese. I haven't had a bet today but if I do I will let you know the name of the horse, the meeting and the odds. I sign on next Thursday at 2pm and thereafter after every two weeks. I receive £73-20 a week and get my rent paid, though there is a shortfall of ten pounds a month which along with the yearly 10% council bill is a tad onerous," reeled off Wes before sipping his pint of bitter. Two-Guns looked nonplussed with mouth agape. "Any questions Two-Guns?"

Two-Guns meekly shook his head and then gave a toothless grin. Mac and the other boys started to laugh. Next it was the turn of The Artist.

"Would you like to hear my itinerary Two-Guns?"

"No, you're alright," replied Two-Guns. "I know that you do fuck all as well."

Mac smiled at The Artist as if to say, *Two-Guns is on one today*.

"Did you see Spacey on the way in?" asked Two-Guns.

"Yeah, the *nutter* wants locking up," replied The Artist.

"Do you think Spacey is putting it on?" asked Mac.

"No. Nobody is that good," replied Wes.

"But I managed to convince the *Department of Works and Pensions* that I am certifiable," said Mac.

"Yeah, but you are a genius," said Two-Guns.

"Here's to genius then," said Mac as he raised his glass in a mock toast.

"To genius," concurred the boys, chinking their glasses in tribute.

Two-Guns left earliest after lunchtime. He routinely went to bed at 4pm in the afternoon and was always up at dawn ready for another early morning session. Wes and The Artist, so called because he had once self-published a novel that sold three copies, normally returned to their respective flats in the mid afternoon in an attempt to eke out their meagre funds until next pay day. It was Mac who habitually remained in the

Lloyd's Bar after the others had gone home. If he had a win on the horses he might even stay until throwing out time, but he was essentially a day time drinker. Night time was for the kids looking for excitement and someone to go home with. In winter the darkness would edge in at 4pm, an hour before Dora's opened up and workers started to drift into *Lloyd's Bar*. *Lloyd's Bar* had an early shift and a late shift with different clienteles.

Chapter 2

Blueberry's was a huge grocery store that sold everything from foodstuffs and clothes to pharmaceuticals and televisions. The only thing they didn't sell could be bought over the road at Dora's. It was the focal point in *Fallowfield* that drew shoppers, shop lifters, beggars and lunatics, the biggest of all being Kevin Spacey. *Blueberry's* was open all hours just like *Lloyd's Bar*. There were two entrances to *Blueberry's*; one at the front on *Wilmslow Road* and a rear door that serviced a large customer car park. The stressed and overworked security team pitted their wits against the numerous thieves trying to second guess which escape route they would use. There were not enough guards to man both and the police did not turn up if thefts were under a hundred pounds in value. Turnover of security staff was high. The guards knew who the thieves were but it was difficult to catch them in the act. They should have sat in the *Lloyd's Bar* as that was where most of the stolen contraband ended up, being sold at knock down prices in exchange for drug money. Most of the shop lifters had *class A* habits to feed. Mac and the boys were watching as Mike the Dip exited *Blueberry's* and crossed over to *Lloyd's*. Instinctively they started to check their pockets for spare change.

"Anybody want to buy some meat?" asked Mike the Dip, a skinny looking reprobate of thirty something years and inveterate tatterdemalion.

"How much?" asked Mac.

"Three steaks for a tenner."

"Let's have a look," said Two-Guns.

Mike the Dip passed a heavy looking plastic bag over. Two-Guns examined the meat without removing the items from the bag.

"I will take the lot for fifteen quid," announced Two-Guns.

"But there are six steaks," said Mike the Dip.

"Fifteen quid, cash money," repeated Two-Guns.

Mike the Dip pretended to hesitate but everyone present knew he would accept the offer. He was that desperate.

"Okay, fifteen quid, but you are getting a heck of a deal."

Two-Guns discretely passed the money over in exchange for the bag. Mike the Dip nodded farewell and turned on his heels. Mac and the boys smiled as Mike the Dip crossed the road and marched straight back into *Blueberry's*.

"He will get caught," predicted The Artist.

"He gets caught all the time," said Mac. "They just tell him to stay out for a week."

"Looks like you got a good deal there," said Wes.

"Yeah, *lovely Jubilee*," smiled Two-Guns.

"What time am I coming round for tea?" asked Mac.

"No chance," replied Two-Guns. "I am going to be eating steak all week!"

"Fat little bastard," spat Mac.

"You're only jealous," grinned Two-Guns.

"I don't buy anything off the Dip," said Mac. "He stole my neighbour's hanging baskets."

"Look at Spacey now," interjected The Artist changing the subject.

As Mac and the boys looked out of the window Kevin Spacey rode past hanging on to the back of a council garbage truck waving his free arm in a regal fashion.

Mac and the boys had known each other for years, which was just as well as Two-Guns asked all the questions. His back story would never have emerged if he hadn't lived in the area all his life and wasn't so well known. Two-Guns knew everything about his mates apart from their *National Insurance* numbers. He forgot most of the answers to the questions he asked, but over the years he had guilelessly absorbed a wealth of information when it came to the personal details of Mac and the boys. Two-Guns had no agenda, he just liked asking questions.

Mac was the unelected leader and mentor of this group of men with no ambition these days beyond food, drink and contentment. He had worked for a few months as a builder on a Cumbrian nuclear power station but for most of his life he had lived by his wits. As a young man Mac had soldiered on the street but with maturity he now preferred to buy and sell goods and bet on the horses, using *Lloyd's Bar* as his office. If he maintained his charade and kept his nose clean the authorities shouldn't be a problem. There were already signs that the *Department of Work and Pensions* had written him off as a mad man.

In contrast Wes had worked legitimately most of his adult life with twenty years at the gas board and then voluntary redundancy; the lump sum pay off long since spent. Like The Artist he now signed on and received *Job Seeker's Allowance*. They had to spend several hours a week applying for jobs online that either didn't exist, had been already taken, or they had no chance of realistically getting. It was a big enough struggle learning how to use the latest mobile phones let alone cope with the intricacies of *Universal Job Search*. Both men were usually broke but still managed to get in the *Lloyd's* every day for a couple of pints. Wes did the occasional gas supply connection job for a few quid and The Artist had a very understanding girlfriend who helped him out financially. The Artist had tried his hand as a novelist and as a painter knocking out oils on canvas but had failed on both counts. Now an inveterate alcoholic his nickname was more a reference to his dipsomania.

Chapter 3

Mac and the boys had given up trying to impress other people but they had to play by the rules in *Lloyd's Bar*. They knew that the manager wanted them out but were united in their determination not to give him a reason. They also knew that he begrudgingly needed their day time custom when business was quiet. Mac gazed at the traffic on *Wilmslow Road*.

"I've just seen a *Ferrari* and an *Aston Martin* go by," he stated.

"Some people are doing nicely," said Wes.

"Nearly as well as Two-Guns," interjected The Artist.

"Fuck off," replied Two-Guns. "I haven't got much but what I have got I have worked for, unlike some."

"What are you trying to say?" asked Wes.

"I wasn't referring to you," replied Two-Guns.

"He was talking about me," said The Artist.

"Well, if the cap fits," said Two-Guns.

"You've rewritten history, Two-Guns. I don't remember you working that long on the railways. You're just as bone idle as everyone else you bloody hypocrite," retorted The Artist.

"I worked at the railway for twenty years. I didn't miss a day. Get a job you bum," replied two-Guns angrily.

"Yeah, yeah, you're a bloody hero," said The Artist.

"Okay ladies tone it down. We don't want to get barred now do we?" reasoned Mac.

"You're right," said The Artist. "Let's change the subject and for your information Two-Guns I have a job interview next week."

"Who is that with then?" asked Two-Guns.

"*The Department of Work and Pensions*," replied The Artist.

"Seriously?" asked Mac.

"Yeah, next Wednesday at 9-30am, before you ask two-Guns," confirmed The Artist.

"You've got no chance," said Wes.

"I agree," replied The Artist. "I've used Two-Guns as one of my references."

"You're definitely fucked then," said Mac.

Mac and the boys started to laugh. The manager and the young female student behind the bar heard the noise and looked over with disapproving expressions.

"Easy boys. We don't want anyone to think that we are enjoying ourselves," said Mac.

The boys nodded in agreement as Mac gave a friendly wave to the manager.

"You shouldn't be so hard on The Artist, Two-Guns. You know how hard it is to get a decent job," said Mac.

"Aye, I suppose you are right," replied Two-Guns.

"And it doesn't help if you have a criminal record," added Wes.

"You're right there. The reason I won't get a job with the Dole is because I will fail the *DBS* check," explained The Artist.

"Why what have you done?" asked Wes.

"Nothing much, just a couple of convictions from years ago. There was an *ABH* and an *Affray*," answered The Artist.

"That will do it," said Mac. "Any government jobs or work in hospitals and schools you can forget with your track record."

"I know," said The Artist. "But I have to show the *Job Centre* that I am trying to find work."

"And most of the jobs in Manchester are public sector jobs so you are...." broke off Wes.

"*Screwed* is the word I believe that you are looking for," interjected The Artist.

"At least you have somewhere to live," said Mac.

The Artist smiled in agreement but in truth it was a nightmare keeping a roof over his head. The Council didn't pay his full rent or council tax and then there were the extortionate utility bills. *British Gas* had even tried charging him for using a gas meter that had been disconnected four years before he had moved into his apartment. At a pinch he could always live with his girlfriend but a man needed his own place. Life was a struggle. Mac snapped him from his reverie with one of his characteristic monologues which usually served as introductions to a wider group discussion.

"Did anyone read the paper this morning about Manchester having the lowest male life expectancy in the UK?"

"Are you trying to cheer me up, Mac?" asked The Artist.

Mac ignored the rhetorical question.

"Yeah, I saw that. Seventy three for blokes," said Wes.

"It's seven years lower than the average for men in Oxford," continued Mac.

"Why don't we move to Oxford, then?" suggested The Artist sarcastically.

"Nah, it's a load of crap down South," stated Two-Guns.

"He's right there," said Mac. "It's okay for a visit, but live there..? Too expensive my friends."

"How much is it a pint down there now?" asked Wes.

"In the posh areas it can be over five quid a pint," said Mac.

"Jeez, that's nearly as dear as *The Houses of Parliament*," said Two-Guns.

"I take it you don't mean the real *Houses of Parliament*?" asked The Artist.

"You're right, I meant the ones over the road," laughed Two-Guns.

"They are a bit dear over there," smiled Mac.

"Have you got any more good news, Mac?" asked The Artist.

"Well, the article finished off by claiming that Manchester also had the lowest healthy life expectancy in the UK," said Mac.

"What does that mean?" asked Wes.

"It means that at fifty five most *Mancunians* have at least one physical ailment that stops them leading a healthy life," answered Mac.

"Like The Artist's *gout*," chipped in Two-Guns.

"Don't forget my *sciatica*," added The Artist.

"And my mental issues," smiled Mac.

"And I've got a bad back," said Wes not to be left out.

"So we are all fucked," concluded Mac.

"Yeah, but we are all surviving," said The Artist.

"Like the city scavengers that we are, like the foxes and the pigeons," added Mac.

"I've got a fox that visits my garden at night," said Two-Guns.

"Do you feed it?" asked Wes.

"Yes. I leave it an egg out. If I leave anything else then next door's cat gets it but luckily the cat doesn't like eggs so the fox eats that at least."

"Fascinating Two-Guns, or should I say David Attenborough," said The Artist.

Two-Guns slowly rose from his eat and gave a toothless grin.

"I am going out for a fag."

"That reminds me," said Mac. "I've got the thirty gram pouch of *baccy* you asked for."

"Fourteen quid?" asked Two-Guns.

"Yep, as agreed," replied Mac.

Mac handed the tobacco to Two-Guns who counted out a ten pound note and four pound coins before sliding them across the table towards Mac. Two-Guns then headed for the outdoor smoking area.

"Two-Guns seems healthy enough and he smokes like a chimney," said The Artist.

"He's an exception to the rule," said Mac.

"Maybe bums live longer. No stress, no worries," suggested The Artist.

"You should live to a hundred then," replied Mac.

"At least," replied The Artist.

"I know someone who didn't live to a ripe old age," said Wes.

"Why, who has died now?" asked Mac.

"Kapinsky, the bouncer," answered Wes.

"The bouncer at Dora's?" asked a shocked looking Mac.

"That's him. They found him hanging by the neck from the rafters in his house," confirmed Wes.

"When was this?" asked The Artist.

"Two days ago," replied Wes.

"That's weird," replied The Artist. "I thought I saw Kapinsky walking down *Wilmslow Road* yesterday afternoon."

"It can't have been him," said Wes.

As Two-Guns came back from his smoke outside he was met with silence.

"What's up with you lot?" he joked. "You look like you have just seen a ghost."

Chapter 4

Dora's massage parlour was situated next door to *Lloyd's Bar* before you got to the *Handsdown Hotel*. It was known as an establishment run for the benefit of sex starved husbands who wanted no strings attached sex and had a good reputation as brothels go. Frequently checked by the police Dora ran a tight ship and insisted that her employees did not use drugs or drink on the job. The upstairs bedrooms and reception area that overlooked *Wilmslow Road* were kept scrupulously clean and the girls were nice looking professionals recruited from the local area and Eastern Europe. A couple of the girls were studying at the University and only worked part time to top up their student loans; such was the calibre of Dora's girls.

Dora herself was an impressive looking woman in her mid fifties who had been madam and working girl all of her life. She was a big woman with a gargantuan bosom who still received admiring looks but who these days preferred a managerial role. It was her task to make sure the girls had everything they needed to do their job. Each day she could be seen in

Blueberry's shopping for the necessary condoms, baby wipes and oil based lubricants. She also spent a couple of hours a day updating the business's web page informing prospective customers of the services on offer and which girls were on duty, with their pictures and brief biographies posted online.

Dora was taking Kapinsky's suicide hard. Kapinsky had stupidly hung himself but the sad part was he had told everybody he was going to do it. Nobody, including Dora, especially Dora, had believed him. Admittedly he had been a good bouncer who threw out the occasional trouble maker and drunks but hired musclemen were ten a penny. Kapinsky would be hard to replace because he got on so well with the police, the only friends he had along with the girls who treated him like a big brother, and even more importantly Kapinsky had been honest. He had never asked for freebies with the girls or been over familiar with Dora, unlike the cops. Moreover the big *Polak* had known a lot of secrets about prominent men in the community but had kept his mouth shut. What politicians, policemen and rabbis did in their free time was their own business as far as

Kapinsky was concerned. Dora would have to ask Mac if he knew anyone who might like the job. Of course she knew plenty of men who would like the job but would they measure up to Kapinsky. Mac was an intelligent man. Dora knew that he wouldn't suggest the wrong type of guy, some alcoholic lecherous bastard. *Lloyd's Bar* was full of those sort of men. One of the girls who also had a part time bar job in *Lloyd's Bar* had told her all about Mac and his boys. The so called Artist had made various propositions to the young lady who had been amazed by the effrontery of such a clapped out middle aged has-been and had almost said yes out of amusement. Dora had known Mac for years so she would ask him.

Dora really was a hooker with a heart of gold. She paid her taxes and gave to various charities. She made sure the foreign girls had the correct paperwork to work in the UK and met their *National Insurance* obligations. Dora also gave generously nearer to home never failing to throw a couple of pounds in the beggar's hat outside *Blueberry's* and she bought the Rumanian woman's homeless magazine. She was always discrete when she saw one of her punters on the street and was generally liked by everybody. Mac had tapped her for a few quid in the past but always made sure that he paid her back on time such was their mutual respect for each other.

Kapinsky had been such a solitary man thought Dora. She used to catch him looking out of the window at *Lloyd's Bar* next door, staring at Mac and the other drinkers. He told her that he had tried to make friends with Mac and the boys but they had ignored him. They let Kapinsky buy them drinks but that was as far as any friendship went. Mac knew that Kapinsky was friendly with the police so that ruled out any association closer than a nod of acknowledgement or putting up with his presence for the price of a pint. Kapinsky had believed that nobody loved or cared about him and that had been too much to endure. Mac and the boys had been shocked by the news of Kapinsky's suicide but the next day his death had largely been forgotten or at least wasn't mentioned again by the boys. Only

Mac was thinking about who would replace him. He would have offered his own services but at nearly sixty years of age his chucking-out days were behind him. Needless to say, Wes, Two-Guns and The Artist were completely out of the question for such a role for a myriad of different reasons.

Wes was too small, Two-Guns too old, and The Artist would try it on with the girls, maybe even Dora. In the past Mac had considered asking out Dora himself but had heard from a reliable source that she was off men for life. What a waste, thought Mac. She still had it and reputedly was a millionaire.

Chapter 5

Lloyd's Bar was situated between a trendy coffee shop and Dora's massage parlour on *Wilmslow Road*. Part of a two story building with flats above *Lloyd's* had a huge glass windowed facade and door which gave access to a long drinks counter on the right as you entered. Wooden tables and chairs filled the space on the left while a couple of high tables and stools were nearer to the bar. The toilets were furthest into this large solitary room just past the kitchen and next to the back office where the safe was kept. There was even an invalid toilet as in a toilet for customers in wheelchairs. Mac had his own key to the invalid toilet which he preferred to use as it was generally kept cleaner. The floor of the bar was carpeted throughout except for the service area which was tiled and therefore easy to keep clean. Looking back out through the front windows one could see *Blueberry's* store directly opposite on the other side of the road. Inside *Lloyd's* the decor had the look and feel of a smart but functional cross-channel ferry.

The manager was an ambitious young guy who was working his way up the promotion ladder. *Lloyd's* was part of a chain of bars that were situated all over the country. Ultimately Damian wanted an office job at head quarters, planning strategy and making big decisions, but in the meantime he was biding his time throwing out drunks and screwing the pretty young barmaids. He hated Mac and the boys and resented them dragging the place down and lowering the tone. While he had to work hard and put in long hours all they seemed to do was drink and sponge off state benefits. Damian's hero *Jeremy Kyle* was right about the legions of shameless nonentities dragging the country down. At least the life style they were leading would kill them off early and good riddance too. One day he would wave them goodbye forever, the losers. Mac and the boys didn't think much of Damian either, detecting in his demeanour a thinly veiled contempt for both them personally and their philosophy on life.

Mac and the boys were synonymous with *Lloyd's Bar* but there were other permanent fixtures. A couple of veteran Irishman had their own corner table where they sat each day talking about the old country, and there was old Frank and Zimmerman. Frank walked five miles and still supped ten pints a day at the age of seventy five, another die hard character bucking the mortality averages. For thirty years he had worked in a Stockport abattoir and now with a marriage and grown up kids behind him lived for the pub. A man of slight build he wore distinctive heavy framed glasses and sported an eccentric looking Russian fur hat. As a young man Frank had been a card carrying member of the *Communist Party of Great Britain* and loved Joseph Stalin. Zimmerman also had a history more colourful than the predictability of his present life. In his youth he had been known for his physical prowess with the shovel or *banjo* and his ability to dig large holes in the ground very quickly. These days he lived near *The Handsdown* and could barely walk without the aid of his frame, not that that deterred him from getting to *Lloyd's Bar*. Along with the old guys there were last and by every means least the cheeky beggars who shuttled in and out of *Lloyd's* quickly before they got spotted by the manager. Two-Guns hated being asked for money when he was sat having a quiet drink. Begging on the streets was one thing but *Lloyd's* was a sanctuary and being tapped up in your local left Two-Guns feeling violated. He had zero tolerance for spongers in boozers and had told Mike the Dip and his ilk where to go on numerous occasions.

Students made up the non-local fraternity who hung out in *Lloyd's* taking advantage of the free *wi-fi*. They were inoffensive except when they turned up mob handed and started rearranging tables and chairs as if they owned the place. Mac had got particularly irate one day when a group of young upstarts inadvertently moved Zimmerman's usual chair. Mac had dressed them down in a fit of indignation and Zimmerman got back his rightful place near the bar so he didn't have to struggle to get served. The argument had got quite heated at one point with a spirited young lady calling Mac *a sad bastard*. He had retorted with an instruction to *fuck off back to Yorkshire* from whence the fair maiden hailed judging by her accent. Eventually the dispute was settled with Damian for once coming down on the locals' side. Even he had to admit that Mac was right and besides it was a pain having to continually move furniture back to its original position after students had left. Shortly afterwards Damian put up a sign that read, *please do not move the furniture*, a policy that Mac and the boys heartily approved of.

Mac was a well built man of five feet ten inches in height with a full head of dark hair. Always well dressed and neatly groomed he looked like he had just walked off an exclusive golf course. Despite carrying a bit of excess weight he was still physically fit which was down to good genetics and a healthy diet. Most evenings he would dine on steak or chicken with a green salad, washed down with a bottle of expensive red wine.

"If it's good enough for *the Pope*, then it is good enough for me," he frequently joked.

Mac lived by himself in a smart apartment but had a couple of ex-girlfriends who he called on. He had friends in Liverpool,

Jersey and Amsterdam and managed to holiday abroad two or three times a year. Everybody loved Mac apart from the police and the *Job Centre* who both resented his self confidence which at times bordered on cockiness. Sometimes Mac and the boys sat in silence for minutes at a time but invariably it was Mac who started a discussion.

"I must admit that I don't miss having to sign on lads," declared Mac.

"I know. It's a crock," said The Artist.

"They make me go to a place in town twice a week called *People Plus*," added Wes.

"What's that in aid of?" asked Two-Guns.

"I have to sit on a computer for an hour and apply for jobs," replied Wes.

"Any luck?" asked Two-Guns.

"No. Most of the advertised jobs online have already gone by the time I see them," said Wes.

"He's right," agreed The Artist. "I have to go to *People Plus* as well. It lasts for two years and so far they have only suggested one vacancy."

"Don't tell me," said Mac. "The graveyard shift at *Kellogg's*!"

"Correct," confirmed The Artist. "I couldn't have done it even if I had wanted to. Aside from the boredom of making cardboard boxes all day I wouldn't have been able to stand on my feet for an eight hour shift, what with my gout."

Mac and the other boys nodded in sympathy.

"Have you tried getting on the sick?" asked Two-Guns.

"It's not that easy," said Wes. "In the old days if you turned up drunk they wrote you off as an *alkie* and left you alone for months, years even."

"Now they expect people in wheelchairs to work," added The Artist.

"I'm surprised they haven't got on Zimmerman's case yet," said Mac.

"Give them time," replied Wes.

"How did you manage to get a three month sick note and convince *the Dole*?" The Artist asked Mac.

"I did a bit of research on schizophrenia at the library and practiced the symptoms," replied Mac.

"What kind of symptoms?" asked Wes.

"You know, hearing voices and having delusional thoughts," answered Mac.

"What voices?" asked Two-Guns.

"I told them that the *KGB* had implanted a microchip in my brain and via this they issue instructions electronically so that I can carry out their secret missions," explained Mac.

"And they bought that?" said Wes.

"When I added that I have a glider in my garage which I use to fly to Moscow they started to believe me," replied Mac.

"I don't know how you keep a straight face, Mac," remarked The Artist.

"I just think of the dollars," smiled Mac.

Mac left uncharacteristically early that day to attend a dental appointment. It gave the boys a chance to talk about him.

"You have to hand it to Mac. He's one cool customer," said Wes.

"Yeah, he sure is a piece of work," added The Artist.

"Nearly sixty and still wheeling and dealing," said Two-Guns.

The three men sipped on their pints and smiled.

"Maybe we should organise a party for Mac's birthday," suggested Wes.

"That's a good idea but what kind of party have you got in mind?" asked Two-Guns.

"Why not something to eat in here and throw in a couple of bottles of red wine that he likes," suggested The Artist.

"We could get Mike the Dip to hoist the wine," said Two-Guns.

"Good thinking," said Wes.

"What about paying for a massage session for him in Dora's after the meal?" suggested The Artist.

"It would guarantee a happy ending to the party," joked Wes.

And so it was agreed that the boys would organize a party for Mac's sixtieth starting in *Lloyd's* and climaxing in Dora's. They had a couple of weeks to fine tune the details and raise the cash.

Chapter 6

The beggar who sat outside *Blueberry's* during the day slept behind *Lloyd's Bar* at night. Not that long ago he had rented his own apartment and was signing on but then the bills had started to mount up. The final blow came when the *Job Centre* sanctioned him for missing an interview in Macclesfield. The next day he had packed a small rucksack stuffed with a sleeping bag and a pair of socks and hit the streets after handing his keys to the caretaker of the tower block. That had been six months ago and it now felt like some other person's life. By begging from the public he made enough money to eat and buy a couple of bottles of cider. On a good day he would have enough for a bag of heroin which anaesthetised him to the squalor of his existence until the next morning. Generally people were sympathetic to his plight but the odd heartless twat screamed at him to, *get off his arse and get a job*. Some passersby thought he was putting on an act and wasn't genuinely homeless. It was ironic that he was sleeping rough and the nice Romanian lady who sold the homeless magazines had a three bedroom house in *Duckinfield*. Her swarthy looking husband dropped her off at the back of *Blueberry's* in the morning and picked her up at 5pm. She was self employed and received a tax rebate at the end of the financial year. The beggar didn't begrudge her the money she was making. Life was tough for everybody.

The beggar had learned a lot about human nature and survival in a short period of time. Behind *Lloyd's* he fashioned a bed out of sheets of cardboard hidden behind the garbage cans and lay there as warm and safe as he could be in the circumstances. It was always the early hours before he settled down, after the bar had closed and people had gone home to their cosy warm homes. Recently he had befriended an urban fox which now came within six feet when he threw it some chicken bones or scraps of meat that had been thrown in the bins behind *Lloyd's*. It was a magnificent male with shaggy reddish brown fur that particularly liked raw eggs which initially struck the beggar as odd but on reflection made sense. At first the fox had been skittish but now it trusted the beggar and turned up at the same time looking for scraps. There were also local cats and the beggar had been fascinated one night watching a streetwise tom on the prowl. The feline had flushed out a mouse from a pile of discarded wooden pallets and then killed the rodent with cold efficiency. When the mouse had made a break for it the cat had paused briefly as if savouring the prospect of an easy kill. Afterwards the beggar had managed a few hours sleep, pondering the cruelty of nature in his dreams, before awaking and moving on at first light. He routinely stacked his sheets of cardboard against the wall as he had found them and climbed over the rear wall making sure he wasn't seen. *Lloyd's Bar* was a good place to sleep and he didn't want to lose his pitch by leaving any tell-tale signs of his occupancy.

For the first couple of hours of a new day the beggar would sit by a cash point outside a Pakistani kebab shop on *Wilmslow Road*. Sometimes an early morning punter would feel guilty withdrawing a large wad of money from the machine. A couple of times he had been handed a twenty pound note, on one occasion by a smartly dressed middle aged man whose conscience must have been pricked by the beggar's ragged dirty appearance. As the commuter traffic started up and reached its peak the beggar would relocate to his spot outside the front door of *Blueberry's*. *Lloyd's Bar* was open across the road and he could see Two-Guns entering for his daily medication followed by Wes. He would have loved to join the boys for a drink and a bit of breakfast but Damian, that arsehole of a manger, had barred him for life. The beggar knew that he shouldn't have tried begging in *Lloyd's* but Mike the Dip had told him it was a money making opportunity as long as you were in and out quick before the staff noticed. He felt aggrieved that he couldn't take shelter in *Lloyd's* when it rained or just buy a simple cup of coffee like any normal person. It wasn't as if he was crazy like Kevin Spacey. Two-Guns and Wes were sat on high stools and facing each other at their usual high table.

"I see the beggar is looking over. I bet the poor bastard would love to be sat in here with us," said Two-Guns.

"I bet he would. Pity he's barred for life," replied Wes.

"He sleeps at the back at night you know," gestured Two-Guns.

"Does he? Damian better not find out," said Wes.

"Well, I won't tell him if you don't," said Two-Guns.

"Good luck to him I say. It's no skin off my nose where he sleeps," replied Wes.

The two friends took thoughtful gulps from their pints.

"Did you ask Damian about putting on some food for Mac's sixtieth birthday?" asked Two-Guns.

"Yeah, he quoted a hundred quid for sandwiches and sausage rolls for ten to twenty people."

"There won't be that many people will there?" asked Two-Guns.

"Well, by the time Frank, Zimmerman and the other locals have had a feed it might get up to that number. It's better to have too much than not enough," said Wes.

"Okay, if we each put thirty quid in and I'll ask for a contribution from Frank and Zimmerman that will cover the food," reasoned Two-Guns.

"I will have my thirty next Thursday. That's when I get my next *Giro*," promised Wes.

"Fucking hell, *giros* went out of fashion a long time ago!"

"I know. I still call my fortnightly payments *giros*."

"What about Mac's presents?" asked Two-Guns.

"You mean the red wine and Dora's?" said Wes.

Two-Guns nodded. He was swallowing cider so momentarily couldn't speak.

"I've ordered six bottles of expensive red wine from Mike the Dip and said I would give him twenty quid," continued Wes.

"Fuck, this birthday business is getting expensive," said Two-Guns.

"Suck it up Two-Guns, I've ordered it now," snapped Wes.

"Okay, keep your hair on, not that you've got any. Let's say we are now in for forty quid each and counting," replied Two-Guns.

"What about Dora's?" asked Wes.

"I'll give her a ring tonight when she is on duty and ask if she can do Mac a complimentary massage for his birthday," said Two-Guns.

"Good thinking. She is a friend of Mac's so she might go for it."

"I know. Just make sure that you have a spare forty quid next week. That's when we will need to pay Damian for the food and you'll need something for Mike the Dip."

"Don't worry about me," smiled Wes. "And do you think City will win the League?"

"Don't talk to me about fucking City," growled Two-Guns.

Wes liked to wind Two-Guns up about football. It was a season when City looked odds-on favourites for the League with United humiliatingly cast as their quiet neighbours. Wes had stood on the *Kippax* every City home game in the seventies and eighties. Now *the Blues* had moved across town he had stopped buying a season ticket for financial reasons, but was still a partisan armchair fan. Likewise Two-Guns had travelled away with the *Red Army* in the good old days of *Best, Law and Charlton*. Wes and Two-Guns only watched the matches on TV these days but they still argued angrily about football.

Wes was slight of build and had his hair shaved close, his one concession to personal vanity a small ear ring in his left ear. He always looked clean and presentable and maintained his council flat the same way. Since his divorce he had remained single but he still eyed the single mums covetously on the *Nell Lane* estate. On his way out in the morning he would pass them returning from the school run and exchange smiles, but Wes was realistic about his chances. He had no money and was old enough to be their father or even grandfather in some instances so he put such idle thoughts to the back of his mind. A decade earlier it would have been a different story when Wes was working and frequented *The Houses of Parliament*. He was married then but getting a lot of interest from other women, which he hadn't taken advantage of. It couldn't have been all down to money and youth or the respectability of being a family man, thought Wes. Maybe he had exuded a confidence that had somehow been lost, eroded by years of unemployment and a lack of money. Wes didn't dwell on negative thoughts for too long and appreciated what he had, a nice flat and good mates down the *Lloyd's*. After he had split from his ex-wife Wes had ended up in *The Handsdown* for a couple of months which had been a nightmare. Surviving that ordeal had almost scarred him for life. He still liked to joke about the experience with Mac and the boys. Only the other day Mac had teased Wes about his tenure in *The Handsdown* in front of the others.

 "Cheer up Wes. You might still be living in *The Handsdown*," had joked Mac.

"I wouldn't fancy going through that again," said Wes.

Two-Guns stayed quiet. He knew all about *The Handsdown* from personal experience.

"Was it really that bad?" asked The Artist.

"Worse," replied Wes. "The place is full of thieves and lunatics."

"I thought you would have been in your element," said Mac.

"There are thieves and there are thieves," said Wes. "The low-lives in there would steal from their own grannies."

"Drugs!" exclaimed Two-Guns.

"Exactly," said Wes. "And we are not talking about a bit of weed. There are used needles lying all over the place in *The Handsdown*."

"Yeah, you are a lot better off where you are now," said Mac.

"Near all those single mothers, eh Wes?" nudged The Artist.

"I should be so lucky," said Wes.

"You know who lives in *The Handsdown* now don't you?" interjected Two-Guns.

Two-Guns paused for dramatic effect.

"Only that Kevin Spacey!" said Two-Guns.

"I'm surprised he's not running the place," said Mac.

"He might as well be, it's that chaotic in there," said Wes.

"Zimmerman only drinks in here during the day because he doesn't want to walk past *The Handsdown* after dark," said The Artist.

"That's because he's frightened of getting mugged by one of Spacey's house mates," said Mac.

"Sad but true," confirmed Wes.

"Isn't there a resident artist in *The Handsdown*?" asked Mac.

"I heard that too," replied Wes.

"A real artist unlike The Artist?" asked Two-Guns.

"At least I had a go," responded The Artist.

"Yeah, and you were shit," said Two-Guns. "Now you are just a piss artist."

"Ooh, that hurts, Two-Guns," said The Artist.

"You two should get a room," said Mac.

"He's not my type," said The Artist.

Two-Guns puckered his lips and blew a mock kiss at The Artist.

"Joking aside I've heard there's a guy in there who can really paint. He did the mural in *Mary D's* near City's new ground," said Wes.

"I've seen the mural and I wasn't impressed," said The Artist.

"So you don't rate him then?" asked Mac.

"He's not that good an artist. He is good at self publicizing his work, I'll give him that," answered The Artist.

"He must be good then if you think he's rubbish," said Two-Guns. "Fag time."

Two-Guns started to walk towards the door of *Lloyd's* with a pre-prepared rolled cigarette in his hand. The Artist rose from his chair and followed Two-Guns.

"You don't think The Artist is going to give Two-Guns a smack do you?" asked Wes.

"No," replied Mac. "He's probably trying to tap him for a *tenner*."

Outside *Lloyd's* The Artist had something else on his mind other than punching Two-Guns or asking for money.

"How are the preparations going for Mac's birthday?" he asked.

"It's all organized. All you need to do is make sure that you have forty quid next Thursday. That's when I need to pay Damian and Wes is sorting out Mike the Dip for the red wine so he will need a contribution from you for that."

"What about Dora's?" asked The Artist.

"I rang her and she agreed straight away. It's all set for after the sandwiches and drinks in *Lloyd's*."

It was true that Dora had instantly agreed to Two-Guns' request for a free one hour session. Mac had sorted her out with a new bouncer, a big Irishman called O'Keefe, who didn't drink too much and was respectful to the girls. It was the least she could do to return the favour and give Mac a birthday to remember.

Chapter 7

The Handsdown Hotel had once been a salubrious establishment. It had catered for travelling business men and well to do Irishmen who came over to watch United every other weekend. Beautiful mature Elm trees still framed the hotel's facade but the building itself now looked run down and in urgent need of a lick of paint. The previous owner had sold up and after that the *Handsdown's* fortunes had taken a nose dive. Now it was home to Manchester's rejects; the junkies, tramps and discharged psychiatric patients who used it as a convenient base for their operations. Rent was paid directly to the new landlord by *Housing Benefit* so the long term residents had little to worry about. The owner, an Indian entrepreneur formerly of Uganda, left the residents to their own devices and was seldom seen at the property.

The Handsdown Hotel was an unmitigated disgrace. The walls were paper thin and damp and the flimsy doors to the bedrooms got kicked in all the time. In winter there was ice on the inside of the windows and in summer the temperature was unbearably hot as the windows frames were nailed permanently shut. A manager in name only begrudgingly handed out the mail at reception each morning and neglected to check if Kevin Spacey had taken his anti-psychotic medication. There was one bathroom per floor and never any hot water. Mike the Dip was another resident and occasionally *Social Services* referred a single mother and child as an emergency last resort. Women never stayed long at *The Handsdown* as they were continuously pestered by lecherous inmates and re-housed at the earliest opportunity. Even the local homeless avoided sleeping rough nearby for fear of getting mugged. Zimmerman lived a couple of houses down and always locked and bolted his doors in the late afternoon after his return from *Lloyd's Bar*. *The Handsdown* was an intimidating place and had an infamous reputation. The residents sat on the steps outside swigging cider stolen from *Blueberry's* and glared malevolently at passersby with hatred in their eyes. The only person of any worth staying at the hotel was an artist who originally hailed from Bolton but had travelled all over the world. Compared to a pavement in Karachi *The Handsdown* was bearable as far as he was concerned. It was merely a temporary inconvenience which he bore with good grace. Joe was waiting for some inheritance money to come through which would finance his return to New York and a possible reconciliation with his estranged American wife. He had used his time as productively as possible painting a mural of *Maine Road* in *Mary D's* bar near the *Ethiad* which had been well received. Currently he was making a life size man made of *papier-mache* which he intended to wheel around *Fallowfield* in a wheelchair. It would be a good way of getting his work out there and making it visible to the public. A local man who struggled past on a walking frame every morning had inspired the *paper man* project. Joe really was an artist unlike The Artist who was wastefully drinking his life away.

The Artist had been told all about the arrangements for Mac's sixtieth birthday celebrations. All he had to do was make sure he had the necessary money to pay his share of the expenses.

That meant taking it easy on the drinking for a few days which was a lot harder than it sounded. If The Artist hadn't had his first drink by midday he started to get agitated and broke out in a clammy sweat. He wasn't the healthiest of blokes in the first place notwithstanding his self-medicating regimen. Overweight, bald, and short of breath he looked particularly fagged out when suffering one of his frequent gout attacks. The only plus in this limping hulk's existence was his long suffering girlfriend who put up with his daily visits to *Lloyd's Bar*. She only asked for his honesty and not to completely take the piss. She understood his artistic frustration and general disappointment with the way his life had turned out. He admitted being a silly boy when he was younger and running with the wrong crowd but that was the past and even she had a past which she wanted to forget. Now The Artist had his books, cryptic crosswords and Mac and the boys down the pub. All he wanted was to be left alone by *The Job Centre* and to get on with the remainder of his life. The Artist was unemployable and the *Job Centre* knew it. Sending him to *People Plus* twice a week to look for imaginary jobs bordered on the sadistic. The Artist always headed straight for *Lloyd's* after dealing with the *Job Centre* or *People Plus* who made appointments for him at different times just in case he was working on the side, which he wasn't.

"Here comes The Artist," announced Two-Guns to Mac and Wes who were sat with their backs to *Wilmslow Road*.

"Morning gents," said The Artist as he pulled up a stool and took his first sip of lager.

"Have you just been to *People Plus*?" asked Two-Guns.

The Artist nodded.

"When do you go again?" asked Two-Guns.

"Not until next Monday now," replied The Artist who found it difficult to get seriously angry with Two-Guns.

"When do you sign on again?" asked Two-Guns.

Mac smiled and shook his head in disbelief at Two-Gun's persistence.

"Next week," replied a weary Artist.

"What time?" asked Two-Guns.

"Shut the fuck up," said Mac. "I don't know about him but you are doing my head in."

"I am just interested that's all," said Two-Guns.

"Oh, we know you are just interested," said Mac.

"Thanks Mac," said The Artist.

The men said nothing for five minutes as they sipped on their beer.

"When do you next sign on, Wes?" asked Two-Guns.

"I give up," said Mac.

Mac and the boys started to laugh.

"How's the new bouncer doing at Dora's, Mac?" asked Wes once the laughter had subsided.

"O'Keefe's doing fine. He threw a guy out on his first night. Some prick hit one of the girls and O'Keefe got the guy's front tooth stuck in his fist," said Mac.

"I bet Dora is pleased to find a replacement for Kapinsky," said Two-Guns.

"She seems to be," said Mac.

Chapter 8

The Artist had pulled some strokes with Mac in the past. They liked to reminisce about the good old days over a pint or two in *Lloyd's Bar*.

"Remember when I had that job at the *Esso* garage, Mac?" said The Artist.

"Yes, that was a good little number," replied Mac.

Both men smiled and waited for Two-Gun's inevitable question.

"Why, what happened at the *Esso* garage?" asked Two-Guns.

"People used to leave their credit cards behind all the time after they had paid for petrol," said The Artist.

"And me and The Artist would go for some nice meals and buy lots of fags and booze," added Mac.

"Weren't the cards reported missing?" asked Two-Guns.

"I'm sure they were," said The Artist. "But a lot of places like restaurants and off-licenses were not computerised."

"Yeah, you could use a bent card for weeks at places where they used manual imprinters," said Mac.

"I remember those machines. You put your card over a carbon receipt and then manually swiped the details," said Wes.

"That's right," said The Artist.

"Didn't you ever get caught?" asked Two-Guns.

"There were a couple of close calls when we got a bit greedy," said The Artist.

"Like that time when we used the same restaurant four times in the same week," added Mac.

"Well, the Italian food was very good," said The Artist.

"Trouble was two cops from the *Fraud Squad* were eating on the next table waiting for us to use the stolen plastic," said Mac.

"What happened?" asked Two-Guns.

"Luckily I recognised them and paid the bill with cash," replied Mac.

"And stuck the card under the table with a piece of chewing gum," added The Artist.

"Yeah, I went back the next night and retrieved the card," said Mac.

"Not that you stayed for a meal on that occasion," said The Artist.

"No, I just got the card, smiled at the waiter, and left," said Mac.

"That sounds like a close call," said Two-Guns.

"I suppose it was," said Mac.

"Luckily Mac stayed cool," said The Artist.

Mac had made small fortunes over the years with numerous schemes most of which he had forgotten about. He tended to keep money making opportunities to himself not seeing the need for unnecessary middle men, though he was always open to collaborative enterprise if the situation demanded it. Mac had never got into the drug scene because he regarded junkies as unreliable and untrustworthy. There had to be some honour amongst thieves though he knew that in truth the cliché bore little relation to reality. A bit of weed was fine whether you used or sold but that was where Mac drew the line; even the school kids smoked it on the *42* bus. Mac had to admit that The Artist had been a talented forger. After ten minutes and half a dozen attempts with loops and cross strokes mastered, he had any signature down pat. It was a pity that the golden age of cheque book and credit card fraud was over. That had been an era when The Artist's true artistic talent had been given its opportunity to shine.

"Do you remember when I worked in the off-license?" asked The Artist now on a roll.

"I sure do. That was the best *X-Mas* that I ever had," said Mac.

"And before you ask Two-Guns let me explain that The Artist and I acquired several cases of whisky that year."

"How?" asked Two-Guns.

"Use your imagination," said Wes.

"He hasn't got one," said The Artist.

"I'm going for a fag," announced Two-Guns.

Two-Guns ambled over to the front door of *Lloyd's*. People smoked outside the bar where a couple of seats and chairs were provided.

"I wish you were working somewhere interesting now," said Mac to The Artist.

"So do I," said The Artist. "Trouble is no one wants to give me a job anymore."

"Yeah, you're old and fucked," said Mac.

"Hey, less of the old," said The Artist.

"Okay, you're middle aged and fucked," said Mac.

"That's better," said The Artist.

"Look at Spacey," said Wes.

Mac and the boys looked through the front window of *Lloyd's*. They saw Two-Guns pointing across *Wilmslow Road* where Kevin Spacey was the centre of attention. The lunatic was throwing an amassed arsenal of empty bottles and cans at the door of *Blueberry's*. A distressed security guard was trying to talk Spacey down while at the same time keeping his distance.

"*Fallowfield* is going downhill these days," said Mac.

"You can't get the staff anymore," added The Artist.

"To think that you used to have celebrities living round here back in the day," said The Artist.

"Hurricane Higgins used to booze in here," said Mac.

"He lived in *Appleby Lodge*," said Wes.

"I was in the flat next door the night he threw a *TV* out of the window," said Mac.

"What happened?" asked Two-Guns who had rejoined the company.

"It blew up," said Mac.

"Yeah, *Fallowfield* sure has gone downhill since Alex Higgins lived here," smiled The Artist.

"Right, it's my shout," said Mac rising to go to the bar.

Chapter 9

It was the day before Mac's sixtieth birthday. Two-Guns, Wes and The Artist had agreed to meet at 9am in *Lloyd's Bar* to finalise the arrangements, an hour before Mac usually arrived.

"Right, here's my thirty and a *tenner* from Frank and Zimmerman which makes forty quid," said Two-Guns. "Let's see the colour of your money."

Reluctantly The Artist placed two twenty pound notes on the table. It had been difficult getting the money having already blown most of his fortnightly *Job Seeker's Allowance*. In the end he had been forced to ask his girlfriend for a twenty pound *sub*.

"So that makes eighty. Where's your forty, Wes?" asked Two-Guns.

Sheepishly Wes put a solitary twenty pound note on the table.

"Is that it?" said The Artist.

"I'll cover the twenty for Mike the Dip and the wine," replied Wes.

"Not if past form is anything to go by you won't," said The Artist.

"Look, I've said I'll pay it so shut the fuck up will you," replied Wes.

"You better or else," said The Artist.

"Or else what?" asked Wes.

The Artist didn't reply immediately. He just glared at his pint.

"Just make sure that you do," said The Artist.

"Okay, forget the wine for now. I have enough to pay Damian which I will do when he emerges from the back office," said Two-Guns.

As Two-Guns finished his sentence Mike the Dip entered *Lloyd's* and approached the boys. Two-Guns noticed Wes's look of unease at the Dip's arrival. Mike the Dip was carrying his customary carrier bag today stuffed with wine bottles.

"How's it going boys? I've got your wine for twenty quid, right?" said Mike the Dip.

"Wes will pay you for that," said The Artist.

"What's up, Wes?" asked Two-Guns.

"I'll pay for the wine but I haven't got the twenty on me at the moment," said Wes.

"I knew it!" exclaimed The Artist.

"No money, no *vino*. I don't offer credit," said Mike the Dip.

When it was obvious that no money was going to be forthcoming the Dip about turned and left the bar.

"I had an unexpected electric bill," said Wes.

"Yeah right," said The Artist. "Give me my fucking forty quid back, Two-Guns."

Two-Guns handed back the money shaking his head.

"So much for celebrating Mac's birthday," said Two-Guns.

"Fuck it. I've gone off the idea," shouted The Artist.

"No fuck you," screamed Wes at The Artist.

Damian had emerged from the back office moments earlier and had heard the heated exchange which prompted him to take action.

"You two are barred," shouted Damian aiming his ire at Wes and The Artist.

"Don't worry I'm leaving," replied The Artist. "You can stick your pub up your arse."

The Artist stormed out of *Lloyd's* followed by Wes. The Artist turned left towards Manchester and Wes headed in the opposite direction towards *Withington*.

"Good riddance," said Damian as he returned to the back office.

When Mac arrived shortly afterwards Two-Guns told him what had happened omitting the real reason for the row.

"The argument just flared up out of nowhere," explained Two-Guns.

"Well, it's going to be a costly argument," said Mac. "They will have to drink in *The Houses of Parliament* now."

Two-Guns thought it might be a good idea to phone Dora later that day and put the complimentary massage offer on hold. He would ask her not to say anything about it to Mac.

The next day at noon Mac and the boys convened in *The Houses of Parliament*. Two-Guns had already drunk five or six morning ciders in *Lloyd's* where he was still welcome. For Wes, The Artist and Mac it was their first drink of the day. Wes and The Artist were avoiding eye contact.

"Have you two kissed and made up yet?" asked Mac.

"I've forgotten about it," said The Artist. "If I look stunned it's because of the prices in here."

"Me too," said Wes.

"I've had a word with Damian this morning over the road but he's not changing his mind. You two are barred for life," said Mac. "This is your new local now."

"Two-Guns will have to start asking somebody else his questions," said The Artist.

"He already has. He was grilling old Frank and Zimmerman when I went in *Lloyd's* this morning," said Mac.

"I was just being friendly," said Two-Guns.

The Houses of Parliament didn't open its doors until midday. The landlord wanted the local dregs of society to stay over the road in *Lloyd's Bar* so he deliberately restricted his opening hours and kept his prices high. There was a lunch time trade with a few elderly regulars but *The Houses of Parliament* relied mainly on its evening business and the patronage of tradesmen and self employed builders who had disposable income to spend. Well behaved students were tolerated as long as they sat quietly in the corner while there was a zero-tolerance policy to begging and the selling of stolen goods. Mike the Dip was *persona non grata* and anyone who looked like a drug user was refused service at the bar. Mac and the boys hated it. They felt like they were under constant surveillance. At least Damian had sat in his office most of the time and was more preoccupied with getting his end away with the barmaids than anything they were up to.

The only consolation in *The Houses of Parliament* was the roaring fire that was maintained in the winter months. Access to the bar was gained by climbing a small flight of steps which had always deterred Zimmerman. In summer one could sit outside in the beer garden that afforded a view of *Wilmslow Road* and beyond *Lloyd's* and Dora's massage parlour. *Blueberry's* was hidden from view as were the beggar and the Rumanian lady who sold the homeless magazines. Kevin Spacey could still be seen cavorting in the middle of the road bringing traffic to a standstill and being a general nuisance to the public.

"Can I get you a birthday pint?" asked Two-Guns.

"That's very civil of you," replied Mac.

"Your money is no good today," added The Artist.

"Right, I'll have a double brandy, thanks," said Mac.

"There are limits," said The Artist.

"Well, I'll just have to settle for beer," said Mac.

"I'll get you a brandy if you want one," said Wes.

Two-Guns had returned with Mac's pint of lager which he placed on the table.

"Happy birthday, Mac," said Two-Guns.

"Much obliged," said Mac.

He raised the glass to his lips and took a long draught wiping the froth from his mouth with the back of his sleeve.

"I'm sixty one tomorrow," said Mac.

"Aye, that'll be right," said Wes.

Chapter 10

Each day at 8am the manager of *Lloyd's Bar* opened its doors to serve breakfast. Damian had moved to the *Rusholme* branch so *Lloyd's* was now under new management. By 9am Two-Guns was sat on his favourite stool with two pints of cider lined up in front of him. His nickname of Two-Guns had been coined because of his habit of ordering two drinks at a time. He liked to joke that the second drink was for his imaginary friend. The real reason was that it saved him going to the bar every twenty minutes. Two-Guns stared at the traffic on *Wilmslow Road* and then the cleaning lady entering Dora's next door.

"Have you had a bet today, Frank?" asked Two-Guns.

"Yeah, I had a two pound *Yankee*," replied old Frank.

"Are you watching the match tonight?" asked Two-Guns.

"Only on *TV* at home," said Frank.

"Are City being presented with the League trophy tonight?" asked Two-Guns.

"I think so," replied Frank.

"What are you having for tea tonight?" asked Two-Guns.

"I don't know yet?" said Frank.

Two-Guns sipped his cider and felt dissatisfied. He missed Wes and The Artist because they gave specific answers to specific questions. Old Frank was too vague in his replies and Zimmerman now sat with the two old Irishmen in the corner by the toilets. Still, at least Mac continued to use *Lloyd's* early doors. Two-Guns could see him crossing *Wilmslow Road* and heading in his direction. Behind Mac he saw the beggar and the nice Rumanian lady selling her homeless magazines. Kevin Spacey had turned up and was arguing with a *Blueberry's* security guard. Mac pulled up a stool and blocked Two-Guns' view.

"Did you hear about Mike the Dip?" asked Mac.

"Yeah, I heard he had been nicked and was doing six months in *Strangeways* for theft," said Two-Guns.

"The silly boy got arrested outside *Debenham's* in town," said Mac. "He should have stuck to local shop-lifting."

"I bet *Blueberry's* profits are up," said Two-Guns.

"I bet they are," said Mac.

"Are you going over to *The Houses of Parliament* at twelve?" asked Two-Guns.

"That's the plan," answered Mac. "Wes and The Artist should be in."

"Pity it's so fucking expensive over there," said Two-Guns.

"I know. That's why it pays to get tanked up here first," said Mac.

"You know why Damian really got transferred don't you?" asked Mac.

"No, why?" said Two-Guns.

"He got one of the barmaids pregnant," said Mac.

"Who told you that?" asked Two-Guns.

"I have my sources," said Mac. "Reliable sources."

"That will slow the little prick down. Serves the bugger right," said Two-Guns.

"My sentiments exactly," said Mac.

"The Artist has got another job interview," said Two-Guns.

"What for?" asked Mac.

"It's for the graveyard shift at *Kellogg's*."

"Sooner him than me."

"You still on the sick?"

"I just got another sick note, this time for six months," said Mac.

"Did you enjoy your birthday the other day?" asked Two-Guns.

"Yes, thanks to you and the boys. The drinks were very much appreciated."

"No problem, Mac. I just wish we could have done something more for you," said Two-Guns.

"It's the thought that counts," said Mac. "You ready for another pint of cider?"

"Yes please," replied Two-Guns.

Joe the Artist got his inheritance money and returned to New York where he now lives happily with his wife. Some of his work has received critical acclaim, particularly his *papier-mache* man in wheelchair which caused a stir when he showcased it in *Greenwich Village*. The beggar still sleeps at the back of *Lloyd's* and the Rumanian lady is moving back to *Bucharest* where her family have built a huge villa complete with swimming pool. Kevin Spacey is set to receive a six figure sum, compensation for a life changing head injury that he received putting out traffic cones on the *M6*. He plans to relocate to North Wales and buy a small cottage by the sea.

Dora is also thinking of selling up and retiring, possibly to Spain, where she will live with O'Keefe. The Artist's girlfriend is still long suffering but continues to the love her big lump of a boyfriend. Different students come and go but Mac and the boys are the same as ever. City ended up winning the *League* much to half of Manchester's chagrin and Two-Gun's extreme annoyance.

THREE EXTRA SHORTS

THE LYNN EMERGENCY SHELTER: economy accommodation *par excellence*. A review by Robert Williams.

If you ever find yourself in *Lynn, Massachusetts*, late at night, and looking for somewhere affordable to stay, then I heartily recommend the *Emergency Shelter* on *Willow Street*, in the charming seaside town of *Lynn*. Having stayed in *Travel Lodges* and *Super Eights* throughout *The United States*, I think the *Lynn Emergency Shelter* affords a better option for the cost conscious traveller and represents amazing value. For a start it's free.

Admittedly the check in at *4pm* and the rigorous bag search for drugs and weaponry are a tad onerous after a hard day's drive, but the slight delay is well worth it. Once through security one can relax in the *TV* lounge with fellow itinerant wanderers and sample the superb video collection on offer, which includes cinematic classics such as *The Nutty Professor* and *Pineapple Express* (always a favourite with the patrons).

Dinner is served promptly at *5-30pm* in the adjoining dining room, *My Brother's Table*. Again, one has to queue in line, but the sumptuous repast on offer is a gastronomic delight and offsets any inconvenience. The house specialty is piping hot stew with green beans, washed down with *coffee a la sucre* (coffee with six sugars). The atmosphere is relaxed and informal with free toiletries and socks available on request at the door.

The bathroom facilities are compact and cater for forty men, but if one showers immediately after dinner the water is still fairly hot, so I suggest you get in there early doors to avoid disappointment. A couple more hours of classic *TV* and there is just enough time for a cigarette on the verandah while the residents in transition sweep and mop the sleeping area, known affectionately as *the dorm*.

I bunked down next to *Ronny*, who regaled me with stories of his time in *Barlinnie Maximum Security Prison, Scotland*. Apparently the facilities there are comparable with the *Emergency Shelter*. It seems *Barlinnie* is a well-kept secret and also one for the traveller's note book. *The Lynn Shelter* is certainly full of characters eager to share their experiences and a working knowledge of recreational drugs and their properties is an advantage but not essential if one wants to blend into the bohemian milieu and get the most out of the shelter experience.

I will express a slight word of caution at this point. *The Shelter* is probably not for those who need a solid eight hours sleep. During my most recent stay I was awoken at *2am* by a fight that broke out in the dorm, two mats down from my own. *Hector* and *Donny* were settling an old score that had started in the bathroom and finished up in the staff office. After a brief visit by the *Lynn PD* order was restored and I once again sank blissfully into an *Elysian* dream. It hadn't been much of a melee as *Hector* is a former *UFC* champion and soon put a stop to *Donny's* playful nonsense.

The lights are switched on at *6am* and breakfast, consisting of *coffee a la sucre* and croissants, is served. Check out is at *7am*, so it is advisable to pack one's luggage early. *Ronny* and the staff bade me *adieu* and I was soon back on the streets of *Lynn*, refreshed, rested, and ready to face the day. *The Lynn Emergency Shelter* gets five stars in my book and is an absolute must for the seasoned traveller.

X's Diary Extract – Erectile Dysfunction.

15th February 2013

We attempted to make love last night, for the first time in weeks, but the exercise ended in failure. I just couldn't manage to get an erection. It was humiliating. The more she tried the less aroused I became. It's a far cry from when we first met ten years ago. Life was one long honey moon with us falling in and out of bed. She still wants sex but I'm happy watching late night television and then creeping into bed for a welcome sleep.

1st March 2013

I don't know what's up with me. Still no sex between us and it's been six months, so she says. I didn't think it had been that long. There's nothing bothering me at work and we have no money troubles. Maybe the magic has just worn off. I have a confession – when my wife goes to work, I've started watching internet porn. Sometimes I masturbate though it takes a bit of effort. This is as much for reassurance that everything is still working, as much as anything else. Watching porn behind my wife's back makes me feel guilty. It seems I do not have a physical problem *per se*. My inability to make love to my wife must be psychologically based.

29th March 2013

We argue a lot these days, mainly about little things. Why didn't I empty the rubbish bags and why a bunch of flowers wouldn't go amiss every now and again. We are both drinking a lot more than we used to. These days it's the only thing we have in common. They say wine and food are the sex of the middle aged. I think there's something in that. I can't believe couples of our age are all bonking like rabbits. Modern life is just too tiring for all that passion, isn't it? Perhaps celibacy within long term relationships is the last great unspoken taboo? I still watch porn which is counter- productive as it makes me aware of what I'm missing. I wish I was 21 again. These days the spirit is willing but the flesh is weak. I guess it's good that I can still see some humour in the situation. Frankly though, it feels like I'm living in denial. Too much booze and crap *TV* and not enough sex. I dread going to bed these days. We used to fall asleep in each other's arms but now we sleep with our backs turned at extreme sides of the bed. It's as if a *Berlin Wall* has been constructed down the centre of the mattress.

6th April 2014

I try not to think about sex with my wife. I dare not initiate anything as I think my efforts would end in failure. The biological imperative/urge just isn't there anymore. My wife is too old for children and I'm no spring chicken. Is this a natural waning of the powers? Are we both biologically redundant or have I been watching too many wild-life documentaries. Everybody is genes mad these days. We went on holiday recently and that was a disaster on the sex front. Sunshine and sea air did not have the desired effect. We just ended up drinking even more than usual and crashing out. The first night my wife was begging for sex, "seeing as though we are on holiday". Sympathy proved even less of a turn on. For the first time I'm beginning to feel sorry for my wife. She deserves a love life as she's still a relatively young woman, but I don't seem up to the job. This is beginning to get me down. I saw a photo of myself from the holiday and I looked completely hacked off with life. I also looked 10 years older than I am. I've put a bit of weight on but that's natural middle aged spread isn't it?

15th June 2014

I decided to go to the doctor. No sex for over a year. This can't go on. I'm only forty six. I don't even watch porn these days. He took my blood pressure and weighed me. A bit overweight but nothing to worry about and the *BP* was fine. He asked me about work and I assured him everything was okay though I don't quite have the old spring in the step. He prescribed me some *Viagra*. He told me to swallow it quickly otherwise I'd get a stiff neck! That was a joke. Think I'll slip it in my cocoa tonight and see what develops.

19th September 2014

So much for the *Viagra*! It made me feel a bit warm in the groin area but we still haven't had intercourse. I went back to my *GP* and he's referred me to a therapist who specialises in *family* matters. I don't know about therapy. It would be a help if my wife and I started talking to each other. We are now in separate rooms. It was her idea. I've noticed that she's started making more of an effort with her appearance but I don't think it's for my benefit. She goes out a lot now. Do you think she might be seeing someone else? I couldn't blame her really.

Diagnosis – Erectile Dysfunction and related Anxiety

For those aged between *40-49*, erectile dysfunction occurs for *11%* of men and is therefore quite common. Physical causes for the condition seem to have been ruled out by the subject's *GP* though weight loss and a reduction in alcohol consumption would be beneficial. X is able to achieve an erection when masturbating and reports that his sex life has been good in the past. This would appear to rule out psychodynamic explanations for X's condition.

More likely, X is suffering from performance anxiety and the fear of negative outcomes. An individual can become so concerned by the adequacy of their performance or the consequences of potential failure that they distract from sexually arousing cues, and lose their erection. In addition, the presence of non-sexual stimuli is more disruptive to men with the disorder than those without. X needs to desist from watching *TV* or thinking about work late at night. However, it sounds like relations have broken down with his wife to the extent that there will be no quick fix solutions to the problem.

Aside from performance anxiety and the lack of adequate stimulation, there appear to be relationship conflicts, a lack of partner intimacy and poor partner communication. X has bought into the fantasy that performance is the cornerstone of every sexual experience and that a firm erection is the key element of every sexual encounter: views not necessarily subscribed to by a female partner. A failure to achieve this ideal has resulted in X's fears of dysfunction, loss of masculinity, and declining interest in his partner.

I suggest that X continues taking *Viagra* though it should be borne in mind that the drug enhances the sexual response rather than initiates it. Erection therefore follows sexual stimulation, and does not follow taking the drug, as is the case in some alternatives. X reported that masturbation requires some effort and therefore *Viagra* may be of assistance.

The main therapeutic intervention would aim at anxiety reduction. *Sensate focusing* is an approach aimed at taking the stress out of the sexual act (this technique requires the full cooperation of both partners which may not be possible in the present case). It begins with the couple learning to touch each other in pleasurable ways, but with a mandate not to touch each other's genitals. Their goal is to enjoy the intimacy of touch, not to give or receive sexual pleasure. Once couples are comfortable with *non-genital sensate focusing*, they are directed to gradually make sexual contact and to give pleasure doing so. At this time, they are still mandated not to attempt intercourse, nor for the male to try to achieve or maintain an erection (although this typically occurs). Finally, when the couple are comfortable with this level of intimacy, they may progress to full intercourse. *Sensate focusing* is generally considered to be effective when marital relations have not completely broken down.

On a cognitive level, X needs appropriate sexual information and his inappropriate cognitive concerns need to be challenged. However, if X and his wife are to resume normal sexual relations then interpersonal issues need to be addressed. Both partners need to sit down with a marriage guidance therapist and tackle, in a frank way, issues such as intimacy and trust and the loss of sexual attraction. It may well be that X and his partner will have to split but the fact that X is willing to see a therapist suggests that he is at least prepared to work at the problem and try and save a ten year marriage. To get a fuller picture of X's erectile dysfunction and related anxiety I need to speak with the wife, if that is possible, and get her version of events and feelings on the matter.

Corporal Hunter:

Hunter kicked the bucket over. I had been mopping the floor for over an hour and he undid all my good work with a single deliberate act.

-"*Cochon*! English pig. Clean you swine!"

He followed up with a swift kick to my ribs. Every muscle tightened up in my body; ready for a fight. That was what he wanted. If you struck a superior you ended up in dead in a ditch.

-"*Oui, mon Corporal*", I replied.

I had to bide my time and wait, but would there ever be a right moment?

Hunter wasn't his real name. Originally he'd been a Spanish national but now he went by his predatory alias. Corporal Hunter was a complete and utter bastard.

-"Clean you piece of shit!"

-"*Oui, Corporal Hunter*".

Hunter started to laugh cruelly.

I still had my birth name, *Wilson*, English and honest sounding.

The name *Hunter* was English as well but the corporal was dark and swarthy.

-"You English think you still rule the world. But here I am your boss *Mister English*".

Hunter booted me up the backside. I winced.

For some reason Hunter had taken a dislike to me. From the moment I had attempted to engage him in French with *je ne comprend pas* he had started his baiting. *Je ne comprend pas* he had repeated in a camp effeminate parody of my attempt at spoken French.

Today had been the worst day of my life. I had never wanted to kill anybody, until Hunter.

-"Clean it up again you swine, *Wilson*!"

Hunter kicked my bucket over again, soaking the freshly swabbed floor.

I wanted to rub his face in it.

-"*Oui mon Corporal*".

The morning had started ominously enough when the bugle had woken the barrack room up at *4am*. We had fifteen minutes to get dressed, make our beds, and run round to the parade ground, where Hunter and a couple of other burly *corporal chefs* were waiting. Whipped into rank and file by Hunter's baton we waited in the dark for the next barked command. Hunter fancied a ten kilometre run.

-"This morning, we go for a little run. Anyone who stops will be beaten. You cannot stop. Do you understand?"

We were kitted out in fatigues and heavy boots while our torturers wore track suits and sneakers. Off we jogged into the

Marseilles darkness; a motley collection of Russians, Germans, Poles, French and me, the solitary Englishman.

Several of my fellow sufferers started to puke as we neared the top of our second vertical hill. Luckily I wasn't in bad shape. A Polish tramp called *Bedros* fell over and refused to get up. Hunter started to put the boot in but *Bedros* wasn't moving.

-"Get up you Polish vagabond. You think *La Legion* needs shit like you?"

As we came round on a second circuit I could see the Pole being loaded into the back of a truck with blood streaming from his face. We never saw him again.

At the end of the run we couldn't lie down. We had to stand to attention in the parade ground for thirty minutes, while Hunter and the two Belgian corporals laughed. They made one of the smaller lads run for some cold drinks; not for us but for their fat faces. I feared for that lad's virginity as he was a pretty boy and Hunter was eyeing him lustily. Hunter was a notorious *breaker-in* of good looking new recruits.

And then Hunter surpassed himself.

-"You will pick up every small stone on the parade ground and place in a pile over here". Hunter gestured at his feet.

The stones were not much bigger than small particles of dirt. You had to squint in the dawn light to make them out, barely a quarter of an inch in diameter. It was a thankless job designed to crush the spirit in 100 degrees of heat.

Hunter made sure we didn't slack. Slackers were kicked as they bent over to retrieve a stone.

-"Why are you slowing down, *asshole*? I didn't say you could rest up."

As the morning heat started to sizzle, and the *cicadas* could be heard in the bushes, we went about our task as Hunter and his sidekicks sat in the shade, guzzling a succession of soft drinks.

-"Work you bastards, work! Go faster, faster!"

By midday we had combed the entire parade ground and removed all of the tiny stones. I pretended that they were coins and that I was slowly but surely massing a huge fortune.

Then Hunter ordered that we put all the stones back where we had found them.

-"Put them all back as they were!" Hunter belched.

A couple of the lads started to cry. A German cracked and he started to blub uncontrollably.

Hunter took him away, leading him by the scruff of the neck.

-"Come with me little German *Fraulein*. I have something nice to show you. Maybe a big German sausage?" The fat Belgian corporals laughed loudly at Hunter's crude *double-entendre*.

I later found out that *Deiter* had been given a different detail, which involved cleaning the camp toilets with his bare hands. When it came to sadism Hunter was a genius.

Hunter tortured me and the recruits like this every day, for the first year. Then we went our separate ways, posted overseas to different locations depending on our specialty.

I'm not in *La Legion Etranger* anymore.

I did my five years of hell and managed to get out alive. I could tell you about desert adventures in *Djibouti* and jungle training in Central America, but my abiding memory of my real life *Beau Geste* experience is of that scum, Hunter. The last I heard, he was running a crappy little café in the 8th *Arrondissement* of Paris, near *Tolbiac*. I would like to pay him a visit now we are both in *civvies*, but I know I would end up killing the bastard.

Hopefully an enraged customer will do the job for me.

Printed in Great Britain
by Amazon